MR. TICKLE
and the Dragon

Roger Hargreaves

Original concept by
Roger Hargreaves

Written and illustrated by
Adam Hargreaves

MR. MEN   **LITTLE MISS**
MR. MEN™ LITTLE MISS™ © THOIP (a SANRIO company)

Mr. Tickle and the Dragon © 2005 THOIP (a SANRIO company)
This edition © 2018 THOIP (a SANRIO company)
Printed and published under licence from Penguin Random House LLC
This edition published 2018 by Dean, an imprint of Egmont UK Limited,
The Yellow Building, 1 Nicholas Road, London, W11 4AN

ISBN 978 0 6035 7684 3
70432/001
Printed in Great Britain

Egmont takes its responsibility to the planet and its inhabitants very seriously.
We aim to use papers from well-managed forests run by responsible suppliers.

Mr Tickle was having a very good day. Twenty one people well and truly tickled. A very good day indeed.

But when he arrived home, he could not believe his eyes.

"I can't believe my eyes," he said to himself. "Somebody has burnt down my house!"

Mr Tickle's house was gone. All that was left was a smoking, charred pile at the end of his garden path.

There was more smoke rising from the end of the lane.

Mr Tickle set off to investigate.

The smoke was coming from Mr Funny's shoe car. Or rather, it had been his car, but all that remained was a burnt shoelace.

Mr Tickle could see another spiral of smoke in the distance.

This time it was Mr Clever's house, and very nearly Mr Clever by the look of him!

"I just got out in time," said Mr Clever. "There can only be one culprit. It must have been a ..."

But Mr Tickle did not wait to hear what it must have been. He had spotted the signs of another fire and was determined to follow the trail.

It was a long trail which led from Mr Chatterbox's burnt out phone box to Farmer Field's burnt down barn, and on through wilder, bleaker land, up into the mountains. Soon it began to get dark, but Mr Tickle continued to climb higher and higher.

Darkness had fallen when he saw a bright light. In the distance, there was a cave emitting a red glow.

Suddenly Mr Tickle did not feel very brave.

Suddenly he wished he had stayed to hear what Mr Clever had to say.

Mr Tickle decided to wait there until the morning. He curled up under a bush and wrapped his arms around himself three times to keep warm.

Mr Tickle fell into a surprisingly deep sleep and the sun was up when he was woken by the rustling of the bush.

Mr Tickle opened an eye.

The bush rustled again.

"I know you're in there," rumbled a very deep voice. **"Come on! Show yourself!"**

Mr Tickle cautiously poked his head through the top of the bush and stood blinking in the bright sunlight. He was quite unprepared for the sight that met his eyes.

He was standing face to face with a dragon!

A huge dragon at that.

A huge dragon with smoke curling from his nostrils.

Mr Tickle gulped.

"Hello," said Mr Tickle, in a tiny voice.

"I'm going to give you thirty seconds to give me a good reason why I shouldn't burn you to a crisp," bellowed the dragon, **"and then I'm going to burn you to a crisp!"**

Mr Tickle gulped for the second time.

Mr Tickle needed to think fast. He realised his arms were hidden. Quick as a flash he sent one of his extraordinarily long arms snaking through the bushes and under the Dragon's belly.

Mr Tickle flexed his fingers and hoped beyond everything that dragons are ticklish.

The Dragon instantly crumbled into a giggling, laughing tangle on the ground.

"Ha! Ha! Ha!" roared the Dragon.
"Hee! Hee! Hee!" wheezed the Dragon.
"Ho! Ho! Ho!" boomed the Dragon.
"Stop it! Stop it!" he cried.

"I'll stop tickling if you promise to stop burning things," said Mr Tickle.

"Anything! I'll promise anything!" pleaded the Dragon.

Mr Tickle stopped tickling and looked the Dragon squarely in the eye.

"What you need to learn," said Mr Tickle, "is to put your fire breathing to good use. You should be using your extraordinary skills to make people happy. I'll show you."

The Dragon lay down on the ground and Mr Tickle hopped on his back. Then the Dragon shook out his great wings and took off, circling high over the mountains and swooping down to the distant valleys.

They flew lower and lower, passing over barns and cottages.

"Look!" cried Mr Tickle. "It's Little Miss Splendid's house. I have an idea for your first good deed!"

Mr Tickle and the Dragon stood beside Little Miss Splendid's swimming pool.

"It is too cold today to swim in Little Miss Splendid's pool," said Mr Tickle. "Do you think you could do anything about that?"

The Dragon thought for a moment.

Then he took a deep breath and breathed out through his nostrils. Flames licked across the surface of the swimming pool. In no time at all the pool was steaming.

Little Miss Splendid was delighted. Mr Tickle, the Dragon and Little Miss Splendid had a very enjoyable swim.

In fact, the Dragon had a very enjoyable day.

He melted the ice on Mr Bump's path, and Mr Bump couldn't have been happier, as most mornings he usually slipped up and bumped his head.

He warmed up Mr Forgetful's cup of tea which he had made at breakfast time and forgotten to drink. Mr Forgetful was delighted. He doesn't normally get to drink hot tea!

And Mr Greedy was very impressed when the Dragon cooked fifteen sausages all at once.

By the end of the day, the Dragon had a big glowing smile across his face.

"Do you know what?" he boomed, cheerfully. **"I feel really good!"**

Mr Tickle grinned and then he reached out his extraordinarily long arms ...

... and tickled the Dragon!

"And now I do too!" he laughed.